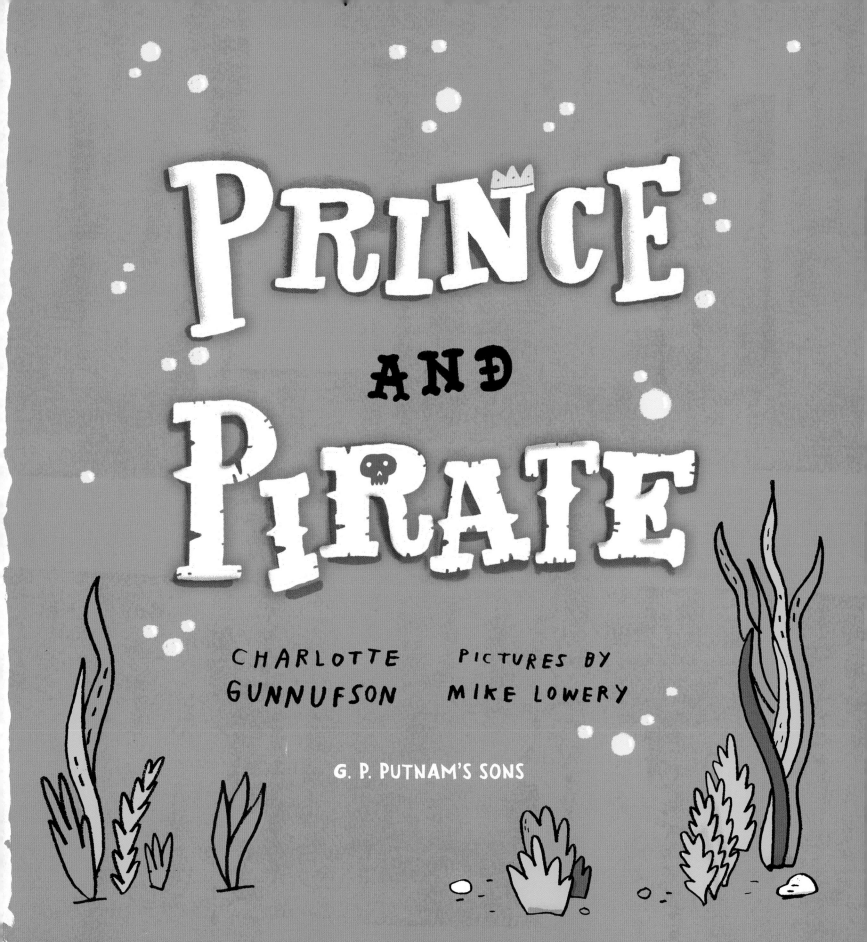

PRINCE AND PIRATE

CHARLOTTE GUNNUFSON

PICTURES BY MIKE LOWERY

G. P. PUTNAM'S SONS

G. P. PUTNAM'S SONS
an imprint of Penguin Random House LLC
375 Hudson Street
New York, NY 10014

Library of Congress Cataloging-in-Publication Data is available upon request.
Manufactured in China by Toppan Leefung Printing Limited.
ISBN 9780399176043
1 3 5 7 9 10 8 6 4 2

Design by Ryan Thomann and Eileen Savage.
Text set in Alghe Bold and HandySans.

For Mom and Dad, with a grand sea
of love and gratitude
—C.G.

To Katrin and Allister and to my
awesome big brother, Jon
—M.L.

Prince ruled a small round kingdom.
He admired his majestic castle and rode in his bubbling carriage,
feeling happy, indeed.

"SIMPLY SQUIDDY!"

Pirate ruled a small round sea.
He sailed his schooner and guarded his bubbling treasure chest,
feeling jolly as a jellyfish.

"YO HO HO!"

Happy and jolly, until . . .

the dreadful journey.

"**UNHAND ME!**"

demanded Prince.

"**I BE HORN-SWOGGLED!**"

howled Pirate.

And the doubly dreadful

PLOP

But, a bit later, when Prince was feeling fit as a fiddler crab,
he realized he now ruled a large kingdom with corners.

"BEHOLD!
I am the rightful heir
to this splendiferous kingdom."

Pirate, feeling frisky enough to hoist the mainsail,
now ruled a large sea with corners.

"SHIVER ME
TAILFIN!
I be just the pirate to
command this grand sea."

Quite happy and keen to explore,
anchors aweigh and oh, so jolly, until . . .

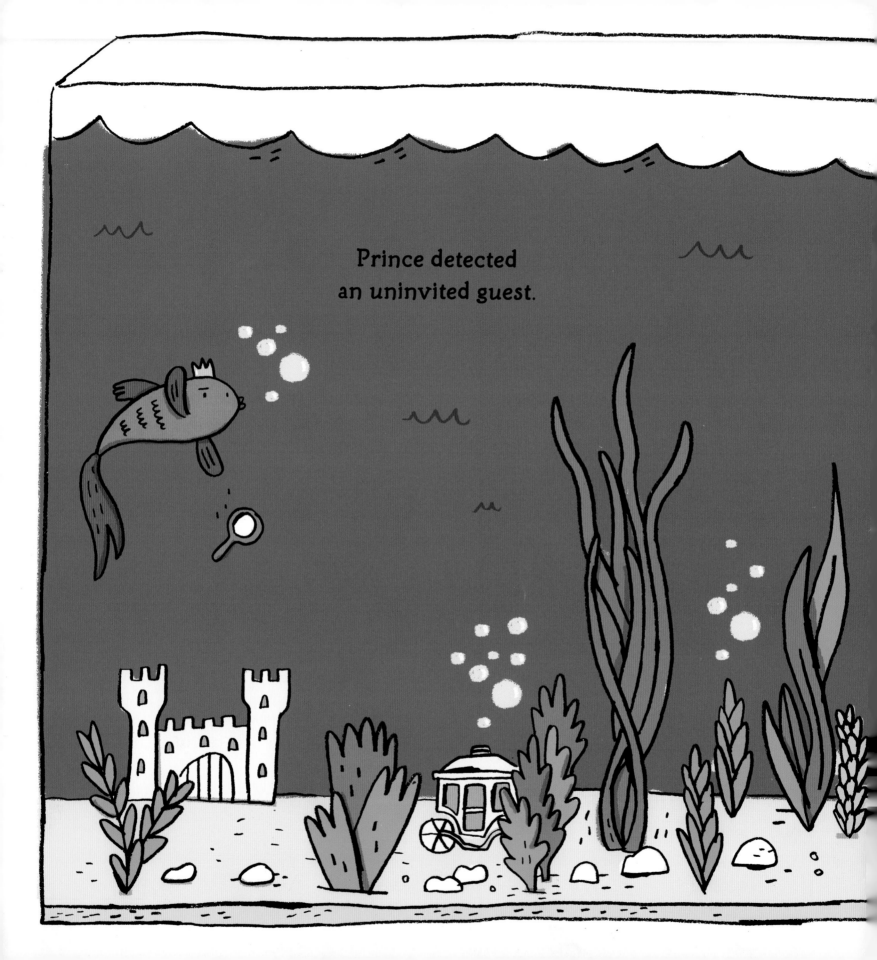

Prince detected
an uninvited guest.

And Pirate spied someone
come to plunder his treasure.

Prince threw Pirate in the dungeon, but Pirate made a daring escape.

Pirate forced Prince to swim the plank, but Prince bravely kept on swimming.

"YE BEST BE KEEPING CLEAR OF ME TREASURE!"

Pirate bellowed.

"EGAD! KEEP YOUR FILTHY FINS OFF MY CARRIAGE!"

Prince exclaimed.

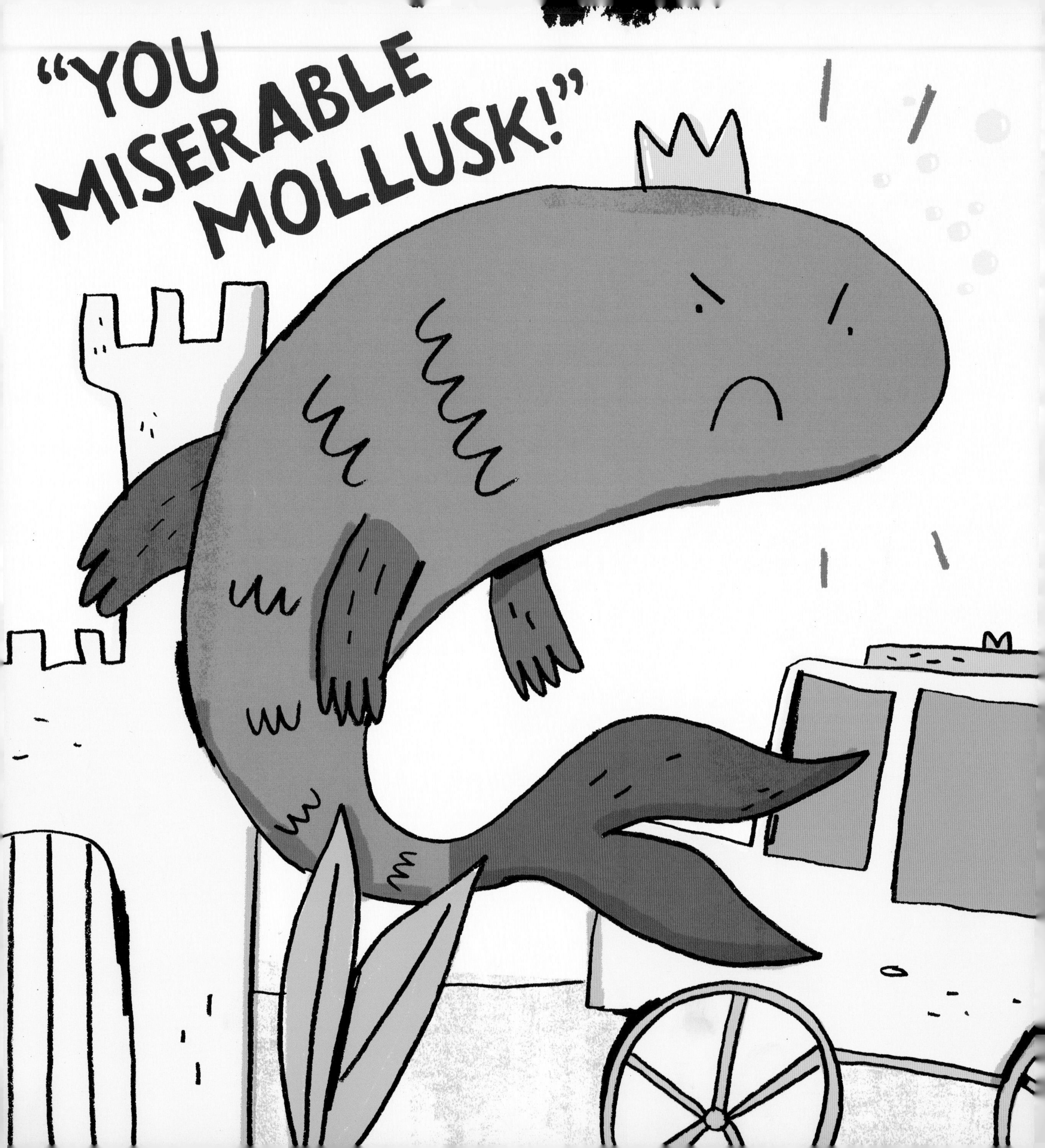
"YOU MISERABLE MOLLUSK!"

At last, Prince and Pirate laid a line of white pebbles down the middle of the tank.

Prince moved it.

Pirate pushed it.

At long last, across a wobbly white line,
Prince sneered at Pirate.

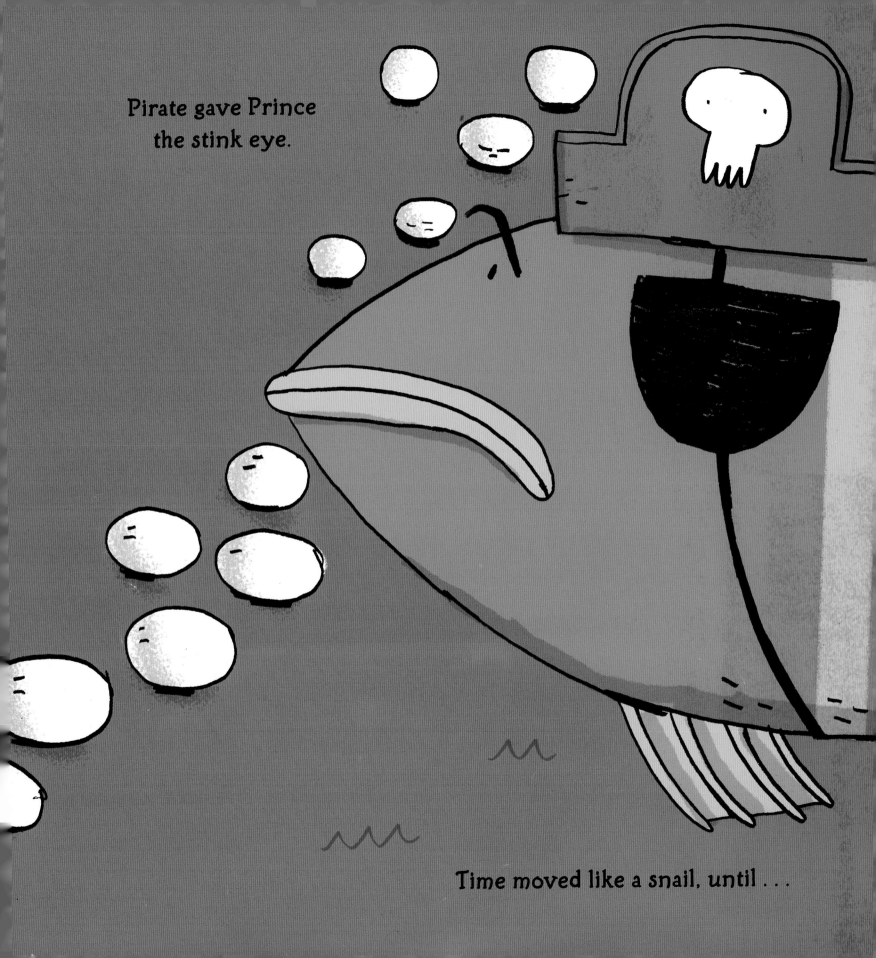

Pirate gave Prince the stink eye.

Time moved like a snail, until . . .

The unexpected arrival.

"SOGGY
SCONES,"
Prince groaned.
"Another intruder."

Tumbling in, tail over fin,
came a lost little dogfish.

He darted about,
then ducked inside his house.

"Poor poochy,"
Prince crooned.
"Don't be frightened."

"Come on, pup,"
Pirate coaxed.
"It be all right."

Prince swished
aboard his carriage.

"Here, boy!
Let's have a nice ride
'round my kingdom."

"Come sniff out all the
treasure in me grand sea,"
Pirate called.

The dogfish looked at Prince,
at Pirate, and stayed put.

The dogfish dashed out to chase pebbles, burbling bubbles, and Prince and Pirate.

"HE BE A FINE LIL' SCALLYWAGGER!"

Pirate declared.

"HE'S FIESTY-FINNED!"
Prince whooped.

With the lively little dogfish,
Prince and Pirate cavorted from castle to schooner,
corner to corner to corner to corner.

Happy, by golly,
so thar-she-blows jolly,
and the teensiest bit tuckered out.